Casey's First Day

Story by Paul Kropp
Art by Evelyn Shifflett

"Keep an open mind and an open heart. Don't take life too seriously — it doesn't last forever, you know. And may I remind you for the last time, keep your crayons sharp, keep your sticky tape untangled and always put the top back on your markers."

— Ernie Coombs

CBCtelevision

Book design by Laura Brady.
Printed and bound in Canada by Friesens, Altona, Manitoba.

Library and Archives Canada Cataloguing in Publication

Kropp, Paul, 1948—
    Casey's first day / Paul Kropp ; Evelyn Shifflett, illustrator.

ISBN 0-660-19241-1

I. Shifflett, Evelyn, 1970—   II. Canadian Broadcasting Corporation   III. Title.

PS8571.R772C323 2004   jC813'.54
C2004-903883-4

CBC
PO Box 500, Station A
Toronto, Ontario M5W 1E6

Find more great
Kids'CBC gear at CBCshop.ca

Casey's first day at school
was coming soon.
Casey was a little scared.

"There's nothing to be afraid of," said Mr. Dressup. "School is lots of fun."

Finnegan nodded his head.

"What if there are mean kids?" Casey asked. "What if the teacher asks me to count to 100? What if she asks me to read a big word like pumpernickel?"

"I bet there won't be any mean kids," said Mr. Dressup. "I have trouble spelling pumpernickel myself. The teacher won't ask you to do that."

"What if the teacher asks me to tie my shoes?" Casey asked. "I bet all the other kids know how to tie their shoes."

"Don't worry," said Mr. Dressup. "Lots of kids are still learning to tie their own shoes. Sometimes I have trouble tying shoes myself!"

The first day of school finally came.
Mr. Dressup and Finnegan said
goodbye to Casey in the schoolyard.

"You're going to have a great day," Mr. Dressup told Casey.

But Casey wasn't so sure.

The classroom looked very, very big.

Casey felt very, very small.

There must have been twenty other kids in class.

None of the kids looked mean, but all of them looked very smart.

The teacher put a big letter on the board.
Then she asked the kids what it was.

The boy next to Casey put his hand up right away.
"That's an A!" he said. "I know all my letters," he told Casey.

Then the teacher put
a number on the board.
She asked the kids
what the number was.

The boy next to Casey put his hand up right away. "That's 8," he said. "I know all my numbers up to 100."

Casey was upset. He didn't know all the letters.
He didn't know any numbers after 18 . . . or maybe 19.
He didn't even know how to tie his shoes.

After recess, the teacher said it was time to draw. Casey was very good at drawing.

The teacher said Casey could go build with blocks. Casey was very good at building.

The boy next to Casey said,
"You're so smart!
You can draw and build
better than anybody."

"But you know all the letters and all the numbers up to 100!" Casey replied.

The boy looked a little embarrassed.
"I don't know *all* the letters," he admitted.
"And I have a little trouble with numbers after 18 . . . or maybe 19."

That made Casey feel a whole lot better.

When Mr. Dressup and Finnegan came to walk home with Casey, they were very surprised. Casey was in no hurry to leave school.

"I've made a new friend," Casey explained.

"So there were no mean kids and the teacher didn't ask you to spell pumpernickel?" Mr. Dressup asked.

"No," Casey admitted. "But I did learn a secret."

"My new friend needs help tying his shoes, too."